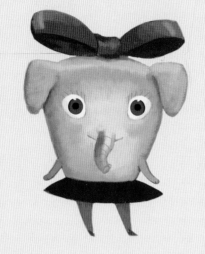

For Hava, Jason, Lael, and Oliver

SIMON & SCHUSTER BOOKS FOR YOUNG READERS · An imprint of Simon & Schuster Children's Publishing Division · 1230 Avenue of the Americas, New York, New York 10020 · Copyright © 2016 by David Gordon · All rights reserved, including the right of reproduction in whole or in part in any form. · SIMON & SCHUSTER BOOKS FOR YOUNG READERS is a trademark of Simon & Schuster, Inc. · For information about special discounts for bulk purchases, please contact Simon & Schuster Special Sales at 1-866-506-1949 or business@simonandschuster.com. · The Simon & Schuster Speakers Bureau can bring authors to your live event. For more information or to book an event, contact the Simon & Schuster Speakers Bureau at 1-866-248-3049 or visit our website at www.simonspeakers.com. · Book design by Lizzy Bromley · The text for this book is set in Circe Rounded. · The illustrations for this book are rendered in Photoshop on a Wacom Cintiq 24HD. · Manufactured in China · 0316 SCP · 2 4 6 8 10 9 7 5 3 1 · Library of Congress Cataloging-in-Publication Data · Gordon, David, 1965 January 22– author, illustrator. · Extremely cute animals operating heavy machinery / written and illustrated by David Gordon. — First edition. · pages cm · Summary: "When bullies try to stop the extremely cute animals from building their sand castle they band together to build something bigger and better"— Provided by publisher. · ISBN 978-1-4169-2441-8 (hardcover) — ISBN 978-1-4814-5967-9 (eBook) · [1. Animals—Fiction. 2. Bullying—Fiction. 3. Play—Fiction.] I. Title. · PZ7.G6547Ex 2016 · [E]—dc23 · 2015011266 ·

first edition

Extremely CUTE ANIMALS Operating HEAVY MACHINERY

Written and illustrated by
DAVID GORDON

Simon & Schuster Books for Young Readers
New York   London   Toronto   Sydney   New Delhi

One beautiful summer day,

Karen, an extremely cute animal,
was at the playground, making a sand castle....

Skyler appeared out of nowhere.

"Hey! Guess what?

This is MY sandbox and I say:

NO STUPID SAND CASTLES!"

He STOMPED!

He SMASHED!

And he walked off, laughing.

Karen's extremely cute friends
were there for her.

Skyler came back with his buddies, Mike and Trent.

Skyler meant business. "What did I say, KAREN? Huh?

I said this is MY playground, and NO STUPID SAND CASTLES!"

The extremely cute animals were undaunted.

But the bullies were watching and waiting.
They brought snowboards, pogo sticks, and **a bad attitude!**

That didn't stop Karen and her friends. The extremely cute animals started building a sand castle that was bigger and better than before.

The bullies SPRAYED!

They SPATTERED

and they SOAKED

the castle down.

Being ... extremely cute ... doesn't mean ...

you can't get ... EXTREMELY MAD!

An hour later Karen came back with the biggest,
baddest, loudest bulldozer she could find.

"Move your butts!
We have a job to do!"

Joshua flew in the
heavy-lift helicopter.

The playground was hoisted away!

Steel beams were delivered,

measured,

and cut,

then

lifted

way,

way

up!

The next day the extremely cute animals opened
the grandest sand castle plus amusement park
anyone had ever seen.

There were roller coasters, water slides, and Ferris wheels, bumper cars and bumper boats, and carousels, a tilt-a-whirl, bungee jumping, and a climbing wall.

Best of all?
There were no bullies allowed.

Until Karen opened the gate,
just a crack, and said,

"Would you like to come in too?"

Skyler, Mike, and Trent were nervous. They knew the
extremely cute animals were extremely angry with them.

But it turned out they were also extremely good at including everyone.

From that day on, everyone had an extremely great time riding and racing, and even stomping and smashing!